THE SMOKING ROOM

Julie Parsons was born in New Zealand but has lived most of her life in Ireland. Formerly a radio and television producer with RTÉ, she has been writing full time since her first novel, *Mary, Mary*, was published in 1998. A commercial and critical success, it has been translated into seventeen languages. Her most recent novel, *The Guilty Heart*, spent six weeks in the Irish bestsellers. She is married and lives outside Dublin.

All royalties from the Irish sales of the Open Door series go to a charity of the author's choice. *The Smoking Room* royalties go to The Rape Crisis Centre, 70 Leeson Street Lower, Dublin 2.

NEW ISLAND *Open Door*

THE SMOKING ROOM
First published 2004
by New Island
2 Brookside
Dundrum Road
Dublin 14

www.newisland.ie

A CIP catalogue record for this book is available from the British Library

ISBN 1 904301 46 0

New Island receives financial assistance from
The Arts Council (An Chomhairle Ealaíon), Dublin, Ireland.

Typeset by New Island
Printed in Ireland by ColourBooks.
Cover design by Artmark

1 3 5 4 2

Dear Reader,

On behalf of myself and the other contributing authors, I would like to welcome you to the fourth Open Door series. We hope that you enjoy the books and that reading becomes a lasting pleasure in your life.

Warmest wishes,

Patricia Scanlan.

Patricia Scanlan
Series Editor

THE OPEN DOOR SERIES IS DEVELOPED WITH THE ASSISTANCE OF THE CITY OF DUBLIN VOCATIONAL EDUCATION COMMITTEE.

Chapter One

Jack Daly always remembered the first time he saw Miriam O'Donnell. It was in Malaga Airport on his way home from two weeks in the sun. She was standing at the perfume counter at one of the shops near the departure gates. The assistant was holding up a large bottle. Miriam was leaning towards it. Her eyes were closed. There was an expression of complete bliss on her small, heart-shaped face.

What was it about her that attracted him? She was very pretty. She had a lovely figure: long, slim legs and a tiny waist. Her hair was black and very shiny. Her skin was smooth and tanned. But it wasn't just the way she looked that made him want to stop and talk to her. It was the expression on her face as she smelled the perfume. She looked as if she was capable of feeling real joy. Although he was never usually very up front, Jack suddenly had the confidence to go up to her. He held out his hand and said, "Hi. My name is Jack Daly. Would you fancy a drink or a cup of coffee while we're waiting for the plane?"

That was how it all began. Within a year they were married. But now, ten years later, when Jack looked at Miriam he could hardly remember the girl he had met that day. She was still very pretty. She was still slim and tanned and perfectly groomed. But the expression on her face was not so much joyous as greedy. She wanted it all and she wanted it now.

As it happened, Miriam's interest in the perfume that day in the airport was not casual. She worked in the perfume department of one of Dublin's classiest shops. She ran the Chanel counter. Chanel was her passion, her greatest love. Of course she knew all about the other perfumes that were on sale. She could identify them and name them off. But none of them, she said, matched Chanel for power, purity or pungency. Chanel had it all, and Miriam wanted it too.

Jack had never been interested in perfume until he met Miriam. It was something girls wore. It was something he might buy his mother for her birthday or for Christmas. He had a few old cans of deodorant and a bottle of aftershave in the bathroom. He might splash a bit on if he was going out on a date. But Miriam changed all that. No sooner had they announced their engagement than she inspected his toiletries.

"In the bin with the lot," she announced. And, as good as her word, she dumped everything she could find. "This is what you'll wear from now on," she said. She pulled a smart but discreet bottle of Chanel aftershave from her bag. Jack bowed his head and accepted the inevitable.

Soon he became good at accepting the inevitable. Miriam, it seemed, knew how to get her way. She had had many years of practice. He had never met anyone before who was so spoiled. It was her father's fault, Jack reckoned. He had married late in life. Miriam's mother had died from a stroke just after her tiny daughter was born. Gerry

O'Donnell had become a father and a widower at the same time.

"Why are you marrying her?" Jack's best friend Tommy asked him more than once. "She's gorgeous and all that. And she's loaded. But come on Jacko, she's a wagon. Admit it."

But Jack couldn't admit it. At some level he knew she was difficult. But she was also fun. And she was different from the other girls he had gone out with. She was ambitious and tough. She knew how to manage money. Shortly after the wedding, she told him she had a plan. She was going to set up her own perfume shop and take on the department stores.

"Take them on and beat them at their own game," she said grimly, as she raised her glass of wine. "That's what I'm going to do. See if I can't."

Jack said nothing. He just opened a

second bottle and filled his glass to the brim. Then he lit another cigarette. He watched her as he exhaled the smoke across the table.

"Mmm ..." She sniffed the air. "I do like the smell of cigarette smoke. Particularly Sweet Afton. It reminds me of Daddy."

There was silence for a moment. Daddy had been dead for just a few months. He had had a heart attack when Miriam and Jack were on their honeymoon. They had rushed home but he had slipped into a coma. Miriam had sat at his bedside for three days and nights. But he never woke up. The funeral had been a high-profile affair. Gerry O'Donnell was a builder of some note. He had friends in high places and they had all turned out. Even the President was there. The first four rows of the church were taken up by large men in dark suits. Miriam greeted them all by name. There was lots of kissing and hugging. Jack was impressed. He hadn't realised that Miriam and her father were so well connected.

Her connections became even more important when she opened her shop. It was called simply Perfume. It was all mirrors and stainless steel, very smart and sophisticated. Miriam, too, seemed to become smarter and more sophisticated every day. The opening was as grand an affair as her father's funeral. Everyone who was anyone came to drink champagne, eat canapés and press their cheeks to Miriam's smooth, tanned skin. The compliments spilled from their fleshy lips. Everything was wonderful, marvellous, fabulous, the best. Jack stood at the back by the cash register, sipping a glass of bubbly, and watched. He was overcome with a mixture of emotions. He felt proud of what his new wife had achieved in such a short time. But he was bemused by this side of her that had suddenly appeared.

"I can't understand you, Jack," she said to him later that night. He was watching the late-night news on TV. A Sweet Afton was smouldering in the ashtray beside him. He cradled a cup of milky cocoa in his lap. "You could be working with me. I'm going to make a fortune out of the shop. The tide is rising and we are going to rise with it. Why would you go on slaving away in the boring old civil service when you could own your own business like me?"

But there was one thing that Jack knew. He was not going to give up his job. Not for Miriam with all her dreams of fame, fortune and success. Not for anyone. And certainly not to become the lap-dog that he had begun to realise Miriam wanted. No, he had decided. No matter what, he would carry on as before. The Department of Health and Welfare suited him down to the ground. He'd started there the day after he left school. He knew everyone and everyone knew him. He had a particular routine and he was happy with it. He liked his desk. He liked his view of the river from his fifth-floor window. He liked the leafy spider plant that sat on his window sill. He even liked the large, untidy open-plan office with its humming computers, flickering screens, overflowing bins and clanking photocopiers. Most of all, he liked his colleagues. Well, workmates he would have called them, but Miriam had insisted.

"They are colleagues," she said.

"Please Jack, it's so important to be professional about your life. After all, you have a wife who owns her own business. Please don't forget that."

Not that Jack could have forgotten it for an instant. But anyway, whatever they were called, Jack still really liked them. OK, he would admit they were a pretty ordinary bunch: no high-flyers, no go-getters, no Celtic tiger cubs. They were fun. They were friendly. They were mates.

He leaned back in his swivel chair and rested one foot against the chipped edge of the desk. He felt in his pockets for his packet of cigarettes. And then he saw the large red "No Smoking" signs which had just appeared all over the walls. Of course, he had forgotten. The new no-smoking rule had come into force. They'd been told at a staff meeting the previous Friday. From

Monday onwards there was to be no smoking in the building except in the designated areas. In the civil service from now on, smoking was next to fraud, making long-distance calls or stealing stationery. In short, it was now expressly forbidden.

Jack sighed and fiddled some more with his cigarette lighter. Then he stood up and pushed his chair back into his desk. He supposed he'd have to do what he'd sworn he never would. He'd have to join the group who went to the designated smoking room down the corridor by the lift.

When the smoking room had first been suggested, he'd scoffed. "Not for me," he said to whoever would listen. "I'll never hang out with that gang. They have nothing better to do than gossip their lives away."

But now he wasn't so sure. He

looked at his watch. It was 11.30 in the morning. Time for coffee, but not time to go out for coffee. He could grab a cup from the canteen. But he'd have to take it into the car-park if he wanted to smoke his cigarette. He glanced out the window. It was lashing rain. There was a nasty cold wind sneaking in off the river. The nicotine craving was getting stronger and stronger. Soon he'd have not only a headache but also a desire to commit murder. He picked up the packet of cigarettes and shoved it into his pocket. He squared his shoulders. There was no real alternative. It was the smoking room or nothing.

Chapter Two

Jack didn't mean to fall in love with Grace Lynch that morning – or any other morning for that matter. He didn't mean to fall in love with anyone. After all, wasn't he married already to a wonderful, beautiful, clever woman who loved him, wanted him and needed him? He kept telling himself this, as he sat next to Grace on a hard plastic chair with an ashtray on his knee. Only the trembling of the Sweet Afton between his fingers revealed what he was feeling.

But what *was* he feeling? He

couldn't for the life of him explain – or explain how it had happened. He had opened the smoking-room door and peered in through the dense, yellow fog. Inside there was an unusual gathering. Smoking, it seemed, cut across the civil-service ranking. The great and the good were here today, rubbing shoulders and stained fingers with the humblest of the office drones.

He squeezed into a corner and dropped down onto a chair. With a huge sigh of relief, he lit up. He dragged the smoke into his lungs and exhaled deeply. He closed his eyes for a moment. He felt the first smile of the day creep across his face.

"Excuse me," a soft voice intruded. "Can I borrow your matches? Silly me, I seem to have forgotten mine."

"Of course." He opened his eyes and turned towards the speaker.

Suddenly he felt as if the world had done a 360-degree revolution. Perhaps it was the cigarette, he tried to reason. The sudden rush of nicotine into the blood stream – that must be why he felt so dizzy.

"Are you all right?" The soft voice now had a worried tone.

Jack turned towards her. "Yes, yes, I'm fine. I just – I didn't have any breakfast this morning. As usual I was in a terrible hurry."

"Oh," again the sympathetic tone. "You poor thing. Here, have some of this."

She held out half a doughnut in his direction. Before he could stop himself, he had taken it from her and bitten deeply into its soft centre.

"What are you doing?" he said to himself. "You don't even like doughnuts. You've never liked doughnuts. And how can you have a cigarette in one hand and a doughnut in the other? Something is going on Jack, my boy."

But what was it about the woman beside him that had sent Jack into such a spin? He just couldn't figure it out. She was pretty, but not exceptional. She was medium height. She had light-brown hair, gathered in a loose knot at the nape of her neck. Her eyes were the bright blue of a sunny sky. Her cheeks were the dusky pink of the underside of a mushroom. When she smiled, as she seemed to do a lot that first day, two deep dimples cut wedges on either side of her mouth. And, of course, when she leaned towards him, first to offer the doughnut, then a paper napkin so he could wipe the crumbs from his mouth, he could see that she had a very beautiful figure. So beautiful, in fact, that before he could speak to her again he had to swallow very hard and struggle to keep his voice under control.

When he looked back at that first morning in the smoking room, he couldn't really remember much beyond the doughnut, the paper napkin and the smile. Somehow he wound up back at his desk, the napkin still clutched in his fingers. He held it out to drop it into the bin. But his hand wouldn't let go. So he laid it gently on the top of his in-tray. He smoothed it out, then put it away safely in his bottom drawer.

That night at home he toyed with his dinner, moving the spirals of pasta from one side of his plate to the other. Miriam watched him carefully. Her tone when she spoke was suspicious and edgy.

"You're very quiet," she said. "Don't you like your dinner? It's one of those special Marks and Spencer's meals. Fresh pasta, if you please."

"It's lovely," he replied, forcing a forkful into his mouth. He chewed doggedly.

"Is everything all right at work? I wish you'd give it up and come and be my assistant. You'd be great at it."

He shook his head, his mouth full, then swallowed.

"We've been through all that so many times, Miriam. I'm happy where I am. Please, just let it go."

"OK, OK." Her voice rose angrily. "I'm only trying to help. There's no need to take that tone with me." She got up and began to pile the dishes into a heap. Then she snatched his plate from under his nose and scraped the uneaten pasta into the bin. He poured himself another glass of wine and took out his cigarette packet.

Miriam sat down again at the table and held out her glass for a refill. "You know, Jack, that I'd always know if you were having an affair." Her eyes held his. He stared back. Then he looked down at the bottle as he filled her glass. "It would be the smell that would be the give away. You know how good my nose is. I can spot another perfume at a hundred paces. You go near another woman and I'll pick it up off you in jig time." She raised her glass to her lips. Then she tipped the rim of it gently to his. "Remember that, Jack. Just remember that."

Chapter Three

An affair? Of course he wasn't going to have an affair. The thought couldn't have been further from his mind. However, he didn't sleep very well that night. He lay beside Miriam in their large bed, tossing and turning. It was bright outside by the time he eventually closed his eyes. Then his dreams were of Grace. The images of her were very vivid. When the alarm went off, and he turned over on his side, he half-expected to open his eyes to her sweet face, not Miriam's.

A rude awakening: was that how you

would describe it? he wondered to himself as he stepped under a cold shower. A dose of reality more likely, he thought as he shaved. He looked in the mirror at his pale face and bloodshot eyes. No more of those fanciful thoughts, he decided as he parked the car in its usual spot. But as he turned towards the office, the first person he saw was Grace. Grace by name and Grace by nature. The words drifted into his head as he watched her walk across the car-park. Again, his stomach turned over and the world spun in a most alarming way.

He couldn't wait until it was time for his mid-morning coffee break and he could take himself off to the smoking room. Again it was crowded. Again it was foggy. And again he saw her squeezed into a chair in the corner. This time it was Jack who produced the doughnut. He'd bought two in the Spar shop on his way into work. Jam oozed from one as he held it out. But today Grace's expression was not sunny. There were no dimples creasing her cheeks. Her eyes were puffy and heavy.

She took the doughnut wordlessly and took a small nibble. Then, with a heavy sigh, she put it down on her lap. She licked the jam off her fingers carefully, like a small cat cleaning her whiskers.

"Thank you," she said. Her voice was so quiet that he had to lean closer to hear what she was saying.

"You're welcome," he replied. "But you're not hungry this morning. Or maybe the doughnuts aren't as good as the ones you usually get."

She looked up at him and shook her head slowly. She reminded him of a small, frightened child – perhaps a child on her first day at school.

"No, they're lovely. It's just –" She put her hand in her jacket pocket and pulled out her packet of cigarettes.

"Here." He struck a match and she bent her head towards the small flame. She inhaled deeply. He inched closer.

"Tell me, are you in trouble?"

She shook her head. Then her eyes filled with tears. He watched, fascinated, as sparkling drops of water crested her bottom eyelashes, then spilled down her pale cheeks.

"No, not me." Her voice was hoarse. "Not me, it's my mother. She's dying. She's just been diagnosed with advanced cancer of the liver. She hasn't been well for ages but she wouldn't go to the doctor. She kept on saying that it was just her age, that she was getting old. She said that I was fussing too much. But yesterday I went to see her after work and she had collapsed."

There was a pause for a moment. Jack watched how her mouth shook, and her desperate efforts to control it.

"Shh," he said. He put out his hand and touched hers. It was cold and clammy. "Don't worry. It'll be all right."

"No." She drew on her cigarette again. He watched the yellow smoke spiral into the air above her head. "No, it won't be. The doctor phoned me this morning before I left for work. He told me it's bad. She's only got a couple of months left to live. That's all."

The tears spilled freely now down her cheeks and dropped onto her hands. Jack pulled a paper napkin from his pocket and dabbed at the wet patches.

"There, there," he said. "Don't worry. I'm here."

Grace smiled at him gratefully. But she knew it wasn't as simple as that. She knew Jack was married. He wore a wedding ring. He had the well-fed look of a man who has his dinner cooked for him every night. And she'd heard the other girls in her department talking about his wife.

"Have you ever been into the shop?"

"No, are you mad? You'd need a gold American Express card just to walk through the door."

"Lovely stuff, though, isn't it? All those pretty bottles – and have you ever seen anything like the way they gift-wrap at Christmas? It's a treat."

The next time the subject came up Grace had a few questions of her own.

"So what's she like, the wife?"

There was silence for a few moments. Then there was a chorus of replies.

"She's an awful pain."

"She's a terrible snob."

"She used to work in Brown Thomas's with my first cousin. The girls all hated her. She was as bossy as hell and fussy about every little detail."

"And how long has she been married to Jack Daly?"

"Oh years and years."

"Any children?"

"Children? Are you mad? That one wouldn't want anything that might put finger marks on her furniture."

"Or make her figure anything less than super-model thin. She's obsessed, that's what she is."

"But he seems like a nice enough fella."

"Jack? He's a dote. A lovely guy.

Great for a Friday night in the pub. Could never understand what he saw in her. Could never see them as a couple."

But they were a couple. There was no mistaking that. Now that Grace had met Jack it seemed that everywhere she went she saw him. Their lives crossed in all kinds of ways. She hadn't realised that they shopped in the same supermarket, in the same shopping centre. They even walked in the same park. More often than not his wife was with him. She was everything that the girls in the office had said. She was small, very petite, with a tiny waist and very pretty in a made-up kind of way. And of course her clothes were beautiful. Grace, who had never cared or noticed what she wore as long as it was clean and warm, suddenly looked down at her boots. She realised that it was a long time since they had seen a lick of polish.

But these days there was more on her mind than personal grooming. Her mother's condition was getting worse. Every evening after work, when Grace went into the hospital, she seemed weaker and less aware of her surroundings.

"It's the morphine," the doctor explained. "We've had to increase the dose and it makes her drift off a lot of the time."

"But she's not in pain?" Grace was anxious to know.

"No, she's not in pain. We have a policy in this hospital to make sure that our patients do not suffer."

But that was not strictly true. Grace could see the suffering written all over her mother's lined face.

"I'm sorry," she whispered to her

daughter. "I've let you down. I should have gone to the doctor when you told me to. I was stupid. I'm so sorry, Grace, that I won't be here to see you get married and have children. To be here for you when you need me."

They cried together that night, the mother and her daughter. But when Grace left the hospital at midnight, someone was waiting for her. It was Jack.

Chapter Four

Afterwards, they would both look back on that night as the night their relationship really began. Jack had a fondness for their first meeting in the smoking room. He said that he could still taste the doughnut. And he remembered the sweater that Grace had been wearing that day. It was hand-knitted, with lots of bright colours in contrasting rows. She said that, yes, she had liked him when they met that morning. And she had liked him even more the morning that she had cried. But when he stepped out of the shadows as she came through the hospital's automatic door, and he smiled and held out his hand as if it was the most natural thing in the world, *that* was the moment for her.

"How did you know I'd be here?" she asked him that night, as they sat in his car in the hospital car-park. He reached across to do up her seat belt, patting it carefully into place over her lap.

"I just figured you would be," he replied. "I reckoned you'd want to spend as much time with your mother as you could. So I just thought I'd hang around for a bit and see when you came out."

"Well," she settled back into the seat, "well, I'm very glad you did."

He put the car in gear and drove slowly out onto the road.

"Your place?" He glanced sideways

at her, noticing how pretty her outline was against the glow of the street lights.

"That would be lovely. Take the first turn left, then second –"

"Right, then past the shopping centre, then turn left again," he finished her sentence.

"Oh, I see."

"Yes, I've been finding out quite a lot about you, Grace. And of course I know where you live."

She smiled in the dark. She said nothing more until he pulled up outside the house.

"Well, Jack, as you know so much, you'll probably know that when I come home from the hospital I don't go straight to bed. I like to sit in front of the fire and have a glass of wine and a cigarette. And I was wondering if you'd care to join me?"

It was very late when he finally

dragged himself away from Grace and drove home. He crept into the house, stopping to take his shoes off in the hall before tiptoeing upstairs. Miriam was fast asleep. He undressed quickly and slid in beside her. And then he remembered her warning. What kind of scents might he have picked up in Grace's house, he wondered, suddenly nervous. But he calmed himself. He had done the smell test. Grace didn't wear perfume. The soap in her bathroom was unscented. There were no air-fresheners in the house. She smelled, like him, of all the smells that went with cigarettes: tobacco, tar, nicotine, paper and the acrid tang of the striking of matches. He smiled to himself as he turned on his side and closed his eyes. Miriam's foolproof nose would let her down this time. He could sleep easy on that score.

But Miriam's mood was not good the next morning. She confronted him at the breakfast table. "What time did you get in? It must have been very late. How many times have I told you not to leave your clothes all over the bedroom floor? The place is a disgrace, Jack. An absolute disgrace."

All he could do was agree with her. He was sorry, he said. But he'd really appreciate it if she wouldn't shout at him. He had a terrible head. He'd gone out with the lads to watch a football match. Somehow they'd ended up going to a club in town. It wasn't his idea, he said. He'd wanted to come home. But you know the way it is when the lads get going.

"No, I don't," she replied with a steely look.

"Ah, you do love. Remember when you were working in Brown Thomas's

34

and you'd go out with the girls on a Friday? Do you not remember? Sure you'd be home with the milkman half the time."

"Not quite, Jack, not with the milkman."

"Ah, you know what I mean love. The odd night out doesn't harm a body. Does it?" And he gave her what he hoped was one of his most winning smiles. She didn't smile back. She just left her breakfast uneaten and slammed the front door behind her. He followed her out of the house. But she had already got into her brand-new Mini and backed it onto the road. He stood on the footpath and watched her disappear around the corner. Then he took out his phone and punched in Grace's number. Now that he had been to Grace's house he could imagine her there more clearly.

"What are you doing?" he asked when she answered his call.

"I'm in the kitchen. I'm feeding the cat." He could clearly hear it mewing. "Hold on, Jack, just a minute."

The cat, an elderly tabby, had crawled onto the bed beside them last night. Jack had heard its growl of a purr as he lay with his arms around Grace and her head cradled against his chest. Miriam wouldn't allow a cat into the house. They were dirty, she said. And the smell! Her delicate little nose wrinkled at the thought. Grace's cat smelled of warm toast, with just a hint of freshly turned garden soil, he noticed. When he got up to leave, just before dawn, the cat opened one eye and watched him as he dressed. Then she rolled over so he could scratch her pale cream tummy.

"There, finished now." Grace's

voice was happy and excited. "How are you today? Did you sleep well last night?"

"No, I didn't. All I could think of was you, my sweetheart." He paused, guilt suddenly washing over him.

"Jack, are you all right?" Grace's tone was anxious.

"Yes, yes, of course I'm fine. Listen, I'll see you in the smoking room at coffee time. Keep a seat for me."

It wasn't too much of a detour for him to drive into town to Miriam's shop. He found a parking space just around the corner from it. He left the car and walked slowly towards the huge plate-glass window. Even at this hour of the morning the city was busy and crowded. There was a traffic jam on the narrow street. Up ahead, he could suddenly see the flashing blue light of an ambulance. It sounded its siren to clear a path. The sudden noise made him wince and the hairs stand up on the back of his neck. A small group of people were clustered together. As he stopped to watch, he saw the paramedics swing out of the ambulance and push their way through.

Jack looked at his watch. He'd be late if he didn't get a move on. He couldn't face telling Miriam now. He'd wait until later. But when he tried to move he couldn't. The small group had become a crowd. And he was jammed into it. There was no way back. He began to push forward and craned his neck to see what was going on. A woman was lying on the footpath. She was small and slight. Her clothes were bloodstained.

"Oh my God," he said loudly. "Miriam, what on earth has happened? Miriam? Miriam!"

Chapter Five

Jack sat beside Miriam's bed in the hospital holding her hand. He couldn't believe how pale and weak she looked. The doctor told him she had lost a lot of blood. Her pregnancy had been ectopic. The doctor explained it in simple terms. The embryo had implanted in Miriam's fallopian tube instead of her womb. When it had grown too big, it had burst the tube causing incredible pain and massive bleeding.

"You're lucky she survived," the doctor said sternly. "If the ambulance hadn't come as soon as it did, we wouldn't have been able to save her."

Jack closed his eyes, feeling a sudden weakness wash over his body. But when he spoke his voice was calm.

"How long has she been pregnant?" he asked. "I didn't know, you see. She didn't tell me."

The doctor looked down at the chart in his hand.

"Oh, I'd say about twelve weeks or so."

Jack tried to think back. Twelve weeks or so. It was before he'd met Grace. Before the smoking room.

"And what about the future? Will she be able to try again for a baby?"

The doctor smiled kindly. "Well, not for a while. She'll need to rest and take it easy. She'll need plenty of TLC. But when she's healthy and back to normal, there shouldn't be any reason why she can't conceive and carry to full term. She'll need careful monitoring of course. We wouldn't want this to happen again, would we?"

Jack sat and waited for her to wake up. He tried to think if there had been any signs that she was pregnant. He'd been so wrapped up in Grace that he wouldn't have noticed anyway, he thought. He'd been so selfish. After all, he was married to Miriam. He'd sworn to love her till death did them part. He had meant it when he made his vows. He had meant it until he met Grace. He had never been unfaithful to Miriam before. He wouldn't be again. Things hadn't been good between them recently, but he would just have to try harder. Maybe she was right after all. He should leave his job and go and work for her. Perhaps now was the right time. She wouldn't be able to manage the shop in her present state. He'd have to do it. He'd have to step in and take over. She could stay at home and rest.

But the Miriam who eventually opened her eyes and demanded a glass of water was no different from the Miriam who had driven off in her Mini that morning. When he suggested that he take over the running of the shop, her tone was immediately dismissive.

"You? Have you lost your reason, Jack? You don't know the first thing about perfume, or selling, or anything much. No, just give me a couple of days to get back on my feet and I'll be right as rain. In fact, have you got your phone there? I just need to ring in and see if that delivery came from Paris. Those delivery guys, if you don't keep hassling them they'll never lift a bloody finger."

In vain he tried to protest that

mobile phones weren't allowed in hospitals. She wasn't having any of it. Eventually, however, he could see that it was beginning to sink in that she was ill and she couldn't cope. She lay back on the pillows, her face the colour of skimmed milk, and closed her eyes. A small tear trickled down her cheek.

"Miriam, why didn't you tell me about the baby?" He took her hand and smoothed down the white skin. "I didn't have a clue."

"No, you didn't, did you? But you don't notice much about me these days." She stared sadly at the ceiling.

He was silent. Guilt had taken away his power of speech.

"Oh, I'm sorry. I didn't really mean that." She turned towards him and touched his cheek. "It's not your fault, Jack. I didn't tell you. I didn't tell you I was feeling sick and tired and awful.

And I didn't tell you because I wasn't sure that I wanted to go through with it. I wasn't sure I could face being a mother. So," she began to sob again, "I made an appointment with a clinic in England. I was going to get rid of it. And now –" Her sobs were loud. Her chest was heaving. Her voice was catching in her throat. "Now I feel so guilty. So bad. So terrible. I feel that I've killed my baby. It's all my fault."

In vain he tried to calm her down and reassure her. She sobbed and sobbed and eventually he called a nurse. He was hustled out of the room. The doctor came and prescribed another sedative.

"She needs her rest," the nurse said kindly to him. "Go away and come back later. She's had a bad shock. She just needs time to calm down."

Her and me both, Jack thought

grimly as he left the hospital. He paused at the door to light up. All around him on the front step were other men, smoking nervously. Of course, he thought, expectant fathers, waiting for the word that junior had made it into the world. How could she? he thought as he left the hospital grounds. How could she do such a thing without discussing it with me? After all, it was nearly as much my baby as it was hers. How dare she think she could make a decision like that on her own?

But she had. As he walked from the hospital to the office, through the city's crowded streets, he pondered. They had both made huge decisions over the last couple of months. And neither had the slightest idea what the other was up to. He would never have thought it possible that two people could share the same house, eat at the same table, sleep in the same bed and yet be capable of keeping such big secrets from each other.

It would have to end, he decided as he got into the lift. He would tell Grace as soon as possible. He had been foolish. His marriage to Miriam had to come first.

But there was no sign of Grace in the smoking room that morning, or at lunch time, or when he went for his mid-afternoon break. He asked some of the girls in her department where she was. No one had seen her all day.

"It's probably her mother," one of them suggested. "You know how ill she is. Grace is probably at the hospital with her. Our supervisor said she could go whenever she needed."

Of course, Grace's mother. In all the excitement he had forgotten about her.

Grace would have far too much on her mind to worry about her bit of a fling with him. He'd wait for a few days before he told her. He didn't want to add to her upset. But as he was approaching the hospital door that evening, a large bunch of white roses for Miriam in his arms, he saw Grace standing outside. She had a cigarette between her fingers. And she was in just the same spot where he had stood that morning.

"Jack," she said, a smile lighting up her face. "Jack, what a relief to see you. I was wondering what you'd think of me when I didn't show up at work today. I was hoping you wouldn't think I'd changed my mind about, well you know, about us."

"No, no, of course not," he began, hesitantly.

"Because I haven't at all. It's just

that my mother has got much, much worse. They think it's only a matter of hours. Maybe some time this evening. I sent you a text message. Did you get it? I said I'd be here the whole time. But I didn't want to drag you down here. It's such a miserable place."

She rested her hand for a moment on his chest, then straightened his tie.

"But, you know, it's so lovely to see you. Thank you, Jack, thank you for coming." And again the tears filled her eyes and gently ran down her cheeks.

"Here," he thrust the flowers towards her. "Here, Grace. I don't know what kind of flowers your mother likes, but these might make her feel a little bit better."

He waited until she had finished her cigarette and disappeared down the corridor towards the lift. Then he, too, walked into the hospital. He took the stairs, two at a time, to Miriam on the fifth floor. She was sitting up in bed, a tea tray on her lap. She still looked exhausted. But her voice was stronger when she spoke.

"Jack," she said, "you've come back. I was worried you wouldn't."

He sat down on the edge of her bed and reached out to smooth her hair away from her forehead. "Don't be silly," he replied. "I'm still here."

There was silence for a few moments. Then he spoke again. "When will they let you come home?" he asked.

She shrugged. "A couple of days, perhaps tomorrow. Soon enough."

"Good." He took her hand again. "It's very quiet without you."

Chapter Six

The civil service was always understanding when it came to family crises. He phoned his boss and told him about Miriam and the baby.

"No bother," Peter Dwyer's voice boomed down the phone. "Take as long as you like. It's a bad scene, the old miscarriage business. My wife had a couple before our John was born. Devastated she was, absolutely devastated."

Jack got the house ready for Miriam's return from hospital. He put white roses in every room and stocked the fridge with all her favourite treats. He was determined. He would have to put Grace behind him now. He would have to make a real go of his marriage. Even so, when he closed his eyes it was Grace he saw. It was Grace's sweet voice he heard. She had phoned him and sent him a stream of text messages. Her mother had rallied. She thought it was the scent of the roses. She was still very weak, and there was no real hope of a cure. But every extra minute they had together was a gift. How clever of him to know that the roses would help. He hadn't replied. She would realise he'd had a change of heart soon enough, he thought.

The days passed slowly. Miriam was tearful and needy. He tried to do his best for her. But half the time she looked as if he was the last person she wanted to see. He checked his phone regularly. Grace soon gave up texting him. And then he saw the notice in the paper. Grace's mother had died. His heart sank. He knew how she would be feeling. He checked the time and place for the removal.

"I've got to go out, love," he shouted up the stairs to Miriam. "I've got a bit of business to take care of. I'll be back in an hour or so." Before she could reply, he had slammed the front door and got into the car.

He found a seat at the back of the packed church. He craned his neck and could just about see Grace sitting in the front pew. When the prayers were over he joined the stream of people waiting to offer their condolences.

"I'm so sorry." He bent down to kiss her cheek. She stiffened and pulled away. "I know I've let you down. Please forgive me."

She didn't respond. She just reached past him to take the hand of the next person in the queue.

He waited outside the church with the rest of the crowd. He listened to the conversations.

"Such a lovely woman. Such a hard life."

"And what will Grace do without her?"

"They were so close, weren't they?"

"Devoted, that's what they were."

"So sad, Lord have Mercy on her."

He waited until the last person had gone and Grace was alone.

"Grace, please, listen to me. Let me tell you what happened," he begged.

"Why should I?" Her expression was stony.

"Because – because I love you."

"I thought you did. But if you loved me, why did you abandon me?"

"Please, Grace, come for a drink and I'll tell you what happened."

They lay that night in the single bed that Grace had slept in as a child. The old cat purred at their feet. A stormy wind rattled the sash windows and stirred the faded curtains.

"I'll have money after everything's settled. The house will get a good price even though it's falling apart." Grace curled herself closer into his embrace. "I'll have enough to give up the job. I've decided I'm going to move to the country. I'll buy an old cottage and grow vegetables."

He closed his eyes and breathed in the scent of her hair.

"Will you come and visit me?"

He didn't reply, just tightened his

grip. Then he jumped suddenly, as there was a loud bang downstairs.

"What's that?" he hissed.

"Nothing, nothing, it's just the back door. I mustn't have locked it properly. It's a bit old and contrary. You have to pull the handle in and hold it tight or else the key won't work. Hang on." She pulled herself away from him. "I'd better go down and fix it. Will I make us a cup of tea while I'm in the kitchen?"

It was way after midnight when he got home. The light from the bedroom shone down into the garden. He hesitated at the front door. He had hoped that Miriam would be sleeping. The air about him crackled with tension as he walked upstairs.

"Where have you been?" she called out to him as he switched on the bathroom light.

"Oh, I just had to meet someone from the office. Some work I'd started before, you know, before you got sick."

He turned on the shower and stepped underneath the jet of water. He scrubbed himself vigorously. Then he put on clean pyjamas. He stood at the end of the bed and rubbed his hair dry.

"A shower? At this hour?" Miriam's tone was suspicious.

"I was in the pub. You know what the smell is like. I didn't think you'd appreciate it."

She gestured to him to get in beside her. He lay back on the pillow and closed his eyes.

"Jack." Her tone was insistent. "We've got to talk."

"Not now, it's too late. I've got to go back to work tomorrow. I've taken enough time off."

"No!" She shook him by the shoulder. "No, listen to me. I've decided. I want to have a baby. We've got to be serious about this. After the last time, I really want this to be OK."

He sat up and reached for the packet of cigarettes on the bedside table.

"No!" She took them from his hand and threw them across the room. "No, you're going to have to give up smoking. It just won't do any longer. Do you hear me?"

"Ah come on, Miriam. It's late and I'm tired. We'll talk about it in the morning." He began to lie down again but she stopped him.

"No, Jack, I mean it. I want to have a baby. I really mean it this time."

She stared down into his face. Suddenly she looked very like her father. He remembered what Gerry O'Donnell had said to him the day he asked him for permission to marry his daughter.

"You want her? You can have her. But if you ever make her unhappy, Jack …"

The sentence had lain unfinished between them.

The next morning Jack was up early. He couldn't wait to see Grace again. He called around to her house on his way to work. She was dressed in black, ready for her mother's funeral. They kissed and he held her tightly. They sat and held hands, drinking tea and sharing a cigarette, while she waited for the funeral car to arrive.

"I'll talk to you later," he said and he hugged her again.

When he got home that night Miriam was waiting for him. She held out her cheek to be kissed. She was looking much better. She had put on make-up for the first time in weeks.

"Dinner's in the oven," she said and poured him wine. He sat down and raised his glass to her.

"You look great," he said. "Just like the old Miriam."

"Of course," she replied and topped up her glass with mineral water. "Now that I've made my decision I feel much better."

He didn't reply. She sat down beside him and took his hand. She lifted it to her lips and kissed it gently. Then she pulled back and looked at him quizzically. "I thought we'd agreed that you were going to give up smoking."

"Well, you know the way it is. It takes time."

She sniffed his hand carefully. "But you're not smoking the Sweet Afton any longer, are you? This is some different brand. It has a much, what would I say, sweeter, more feminine scent."

Jack could see the packet of Marlboro Lights sitting on Grace's kitchen table. She had written "I love you" on the inside flap and put them into his pocket as he was leaving.

"Oh, I ran out today. I tried not smoking anything else but eventually I couldn't take it anymore. One of the girls in the office gave me a few to tide me over."

He crossed his fingers beneath the table as the lie popped out. He would have to tell her. He couldn't carry on like this. He wasn't good at deception. He knew there was no way that he wanted to be with her any longer. It would be better to get it over with. He'd have to be cruel to be kind: but not just yet. He needed to talk to Grace. He waited until Miriam had gone to bed and was fast asleep before he left. It wasn't that far on foot to Grace's house. A huge full moon rode high in the southern sky. Grace's back door was unlocked and he slipped in. She was sitting at the kitchen table. She had a cigarette in one hand and a glass of whiskey in the other.

"You've come! I'm so glad. I'm so tired." She looked up at him. Her eyes were red and sore from crying, but still she looked lovely.

"Come to bed," he said. "I'll make you feel better."

Afterwards she told him about the funeral. It had been sad but happy too. She felt her mother was at peace.

"And do you know, Jack, I was speaking to my uncle. He's an auctioneer. He said I'd get a great price for the house. So I'm definitely going to give up my job and go and live in the country. I'm going to buy that old cottage and do it up. I'll start that organic garden and grow vegetables."

"That's wonderful, Grace, fantastic. There's just one problem."

"What?" She raised up on her elbow and looked at him, worry creasing her forehead.

"Will there be room for me too?"

"Oh, Jack, of course there will. If you want to come with me it would be wonderful. Six months should do it. I've got to wait for probate, then we'll be off."

They lay together in her narrow single bed. The old cat purred. The moonlight shone down on them. Grace slept. Jack stroked her hair and kissed her cheek. Tomorrow, first thing tomorrow, he'd tell Miriam. And then it would be over.

Chapter Seven

The next morning, he was waiting for Grace in the coffee room. He needed the sweet balm of her smile and the soft touch of her hand more than ever. The scene with Miriam had been awful. He had told her over the breakfast table. He hadn't minced his words.

"I don't love you any more," he said. "I haven't loved you for a long time. I thought we could make things work again after, you know, you losing the baby. But I'm certain now, Miriam, there's no future for us. I'm leaving you."

She didn't seem surprised. She sat

and stared at the cutlery, the napkins, the cups and saucers and plates that had all been wedding presents. Then she picked them up, one by one, and began to smash them against the tiled floor. When she had finished, she looked up at him with the face that had become her father's.

"You'll get nothing," she said. "This house, my father's money paid for it. My money has furnished it, painted it, taken care of it. You'll get no part of that."

He didn't care. He backed away from her and rushed from the house. Grace would make it better.

They went home together that first evening. The cat greeted him like a long lost friend. They sat in a cosy silence by the fire, drinking tea, eating biscuits and talking about their future.

"It's so lovely that you're here with

me," Grace whispered to him later, as they lay together in her small bed. "I never realised before how lonely I was."

"I have to go away tomorrow," he said, "just for a couple of days. The Minister is making a big speech about cutbacks in the health service. They want me to do some research in the local hospitals. Just for a couple of days, that's all."

"Of course." Her voice was drowsy. "Of course."

"I'll be back the day after tomorrow. I'll see you in the smoking room at eleven. It's our special place, isn't it Grace?"

But there was no reply from her. Her eyes were closed and her breathing was slow and steady. She was still asleep in the morning when he left to get the early train to Cork. Somehow he didn't manage to speak to her that day. He left her messages. She left him messages in return. And when he phoned the house late that night still she didn't answer. She's exhausted, he thought, as he lay on the bed in his B & B watching the late-night news. Her mother, me, everything: I'll have to work very hard at making things better for her.

But there was no sign of her in the smoking room when he got into work the next day. He took the stairs two at a time to her floor. Her desk was bare.

"Where is she?" he said to the cluster of girls around the water cooler. "Did she phone in sick?"

There was silence for a moment. Then one of them spoke.

"Haven't you heard?"

"Heard what?"

Again the strange and heavy silence.

It was broken by a number of choking sobs.

"The fire. In Grace's house. It was on the news this morning."

"Fire? What fire?"

"In her bedroom. No one is really sure what happened. But it was very bad. She's, well, she's …"

"Burnt, badly burnt?"

"I'm sorry, Jack." Grace's supervisor held out her hand and touched his shoulder. "She's dead I'm afraid. Apparently, by the time the firemen arrived it was too late."

Miriam came and took him home. She was warm and kind. She let him cry and she tried to comfort him. The newspapers were full of the story. It seemed that Grace had been smoking in bed. She must have fallen asleep and the cigarette had set fire to the duvet. The police told him that there was a bottle of perfume on the bedside table. It had helped the fire to catch. Grace had died from smoke inhalation. The old tabby had died too. The house was completely destroyed. When Jack could finally bring himself to visit the scene, he was shattered to see its charred interior and blackened walls. Among the piles of rubbish still smouldering in the front garden, he found a small photograph of Grace. He picked it up and put it away in his wallet.

Somehow he got through the next few months. He turned to Miriam for support and she gave it to him. Ten months later their son was born.

"We'll call him Gerry after Daddy," she said and Jack didn't object.

Miriam was a devoted mother. She gave up the shop and came home to dedicate herself to the baby. Jack was amazed to see her loving care. He was particularly surprised to see her feed the infant herself. He would wake in the night and hear her talking to the little one as she sat in the rocking chair, his tiny fuzzy head cradled against her breast. But Grace also haunted his nights. Often, as he was about to fall asleep, he would see her smile, hear her laugh, feel her soft warmth against him. And sometimes he would wake suddenly out of a nightmare, the smell of burning stinging the insides of his nostrils.

Tonight the smell was very strong. He sat up straight. His heart was beating as if it would burst through his chest and his breath was coming in loud gasps from his mouth. For a moment, he couldn't work out where he was or what was happening. And then he saw Miriam in the dim glow of the baby's night-light. She was sitting on the floor. She had a lit cigarette in one hand and a small piece of paper in the other. The contents of his wallet were spread out in front of her. As he watched in amazement, she placed the burning tip of the cigarette against the paper. She held it in place just long enough to make a neat, round, brown-edged hole. She did it again and again. Grey smoke curled above her head.

"Miriam," he whispered. "What are you doing?"

She paused and looked up at him. She held the cigarette close to her nose and breathed in deeply.

"Marlboro Lights," she said. "Not your brand."

She picked up the piece of paper, held it to the glowing tip again. Then she laid it on the floor and looked at him.

"I thought that I'd got rid of her for once and for all. Well, I have now."

She stood up and walked over to the baby's cradle. She bent down and picked him up. Then she walked out of the room. Jack pushed back the bedclothes and got out of the bed. He got down on his hands and knees and crawled across the carpet. He could see what she had been doing. The small photograph of Grace that he had rescued from the house was now pocked with burns. A sob caught in his throat. He remembered Miriam's words with a dreadful clarity.

"I'd always know if you were having an affair. I'd always know. It would be the smell. That would be the give away."

OPEN DOOR SERIES

Letter From Chicago by Cathy Kelly

Driving With Daisy by Tom Nestor

It All Adds Up by Margaret Neylon

Has Anyone Here Seen Larry?
by Deirdre Purcell

SERIES FOUR

Fair-Weather Friend by Patricia Scanlan

The Story of Joe Brown by Rose Doyle

The Smoking Room by Julie Parsons

World Cup Diary by Niall Quinn

The Quiz Master by Michael Scott

Stray Dog by Gareth O'Callaghan

ORDER DETAILS OVERLEAF

TRADE/CREDIT CARD ORDERS TO:
CMD, 55A Spruce Avenue,
Stillorgan Industrial Park,
Blackrock, Co. Dublin, Ireland.
Tel: (+353 1) 294 2560
Fax: (+353 1) 294 2564

TO PLACE PERSONAL/EDUCATIONAL
ORDERS OR TO ORDER A CATALOGUE
PLEASE CONTACT:
New Island, 2 Brookside, Dundrum
Road, Dundrum,
Dublin 14, Ireland.
Tel: (+353 1) 298 6867/298 3411
Fax: (+353 1) 298 7912
www.newisland.ie